DEDICATION

DEDICATED TO MY BROTHER,
WILLIAM H. ADAMS
FEBRUARY 28, 1938-DECEMBER 24, 1997

ACKNOWLEDGEMENTS

First and foremost, I thank my Lord and Savior, Jesus Christ,
for it is about His love that I have written.

My deepest thanks to my wonderful church family for your love and
acceptance of each other. To Rev. Fred Arnold, thank you for encouraging each
of us to share God-given talents, no matter how small we think they are.

To my wonderful husband, Lee, thank you for your love and support and for
sharing your faith that anything is possible through Christ.

PARKHURST BROTHERS, INC., PUBLISHERS

© Text copyright 2012 by Shirley A. Taylor and © Illustrations copyright 2012 Wendell E. Hall. All rights reserved. No part of this book may be reproduced in any form, except for brief passages quoted within reviews, without the express prior written consent of Permissions Director, Parkhurst Brothers, Inc., Publishers, Inc.

www.parkhurstbrothers.com

Parkhurst Brothers books are distributed to the trade through the Chicago Distribution Center, and may be ordered through Ingram Book Company, Baker & Taylor, Follett Library Resources and other book industry wholesalers. To order from Chicago's Chicago Distribution Center, phone 1-800-621-2736 or send a fax to 800-621-8476. Copies of this and other Parkhurst Brothers Inc., Publishers titles are available to organizations and corporations for purchase in quantity by contacting the Special Sales Department at our home office location, listed on our web site. Manuscript submission guidelines for this publishing company are available at our web site.

Printed in Canada

First Edition, 2012

2012 2013 2014 2015   12 11 10 9 8 7 6 5 4 3 2 1

Library of Congress Cataloging-in-Publication Data

Taylor, Shirley A., 1919-
The Stable Boy / Shirley A. Taylor.
    p. cm.
 Summary: Homeless and mute since his mother's death in Bethlehem two years earlier, an eight-year-old known only as the Stable Boy witnesses the birth of the Messiah.
 ISBN 978-1-935166-79-5
 1. Jesus Christ--Nativity--Juvenile fiction. [1. Jesus Christ--Nativity--Fiction. 2. Homeless persons--Fiction. 3. Orphans--Fiction. 4. Selective mutism--Fiction. 5. Bethlehem--Fiction.] I. Title.
PZ7.T217852St 2012
[E]--dc23
                    HYPERLINK "tel:2012006725" 2012006725

This book is printed on archival-quality paper that meets requirements of the American National Standard for Information Sciences, Permanence of Paper, Printed Library Materials, ANSI Z39.48-1984.

Illustrations throughout, plus cover and page design: Wendell E. Hall
Acquired for Parkhurst Brothers Inc., Publishers by: Ted Parkhurst
Proofreader: Barbara Paddack
122012

Hundreds of years ago, in a little town called Bethlehem, a boy lived with his mother. His father had been sick and died, leaving the boy and his mother completely alone, with no home and no family to care for them. The mother found work with the innkeepers of Bethlehem, cooking, cleaning and lugging water jugs from the public wells for drinking and washing.

Her days were long and her work tiring, and she was paid nothing: no money, only a little food and a loft for sleeping above the stable.

The boy made friends with cows, baby chicks, and a donkey called Josephine. Cats were his favorites, especially their babies. His mother taught him to hold the kittens with gentle hands and to treat each living creature with kindness.

Evenings belonged only to the boy and his mother. She cradled him in her arms and covered him with hay for warmth.

On moonlit nights, the mother would open a loft door. As they gazed at the beautiful stars in the heavens, she told him stories she had heard as a child, that the prophets foretold of the Messiah King who would soon come to save the world.

"Son," she said, "the Messiah will be sent by God to bring peace and hope. He will bring everlasting life for all people—even for the poor like us. He will save all people from their sins. The Messiah will change our lives."

As he dropped off to sleep, the boy asked, "Mama, how will God know where we are so the Messiah King can find us? We have no home, and our stable has no name."

"Look up at the heavens, my love," she replied. "See all those stars? God knows every single one, and He knows where each will be tomorrow night and the night after and forever after that. I don't think He will have any trouble finding a mama and her little boy."

When the boy turned six years old, he could feed the cows and donkeys. He could clean the stables. Sometimes he gathered eggs from the nests, even though the hens squawked loudly and pecked his hands. Many times, the innkeepers told him what a good job he did. His mother felt very proud.

"Someday, Mama," said the boy, "when I am big, I will make you even more proud. I will have my very own inn. We will live there and you will sleep in a real bed."

Early one morning, the boy woke to find his mother lying very still in the hay next to him. She was beautiful. A peaceful smile shone on her face.

"Wake up, Mama," he said as he shook her arm. She did not move. He shook her harder.

"Mama, wake up. Please, please wake up!" he cried. Still, she did not move.

The stable door opened, and the innkeeper called, "Boy, where are you and your mama? Come! The sun is up, and there is much work to be done."

The boy darted to a corner and curled up into a tiny ball, completely hidden by mounds of hay. He remained there, quiet as a mouse. People gathered around his precious mother, who still had not moved. He peeked through the hay, just enough to see them cover her with a large white cloth and carry her away. Somehow he knew she would never return. From that sad day, the little boy spoke not a single word.

For the next two years, he wandered the streets and alleys of Bethlehem. To eat, he stole food. He took clothing that had been laid out in the sun to dry. Some days a kind person would offer him a piece of bread.

Some let him pick fruit from their trees, knowing he was hungry and alone.

He became faster than lightning at grabbing bones thrown from kitchen doors. He growled fiercely at dogs that raced him to the tasty treats.

As darkness crept over the city each evening, he slipped into the nearest stable, and made his bed in the hay. To the people of Bethlehem, he became known as the Stable Boy. Not one person knew his name.

The Stable Boy had hair as dark as soot. His eyes were as black as coal. They looked out from a little round face browned by the sun, or was that dirt? Did he ever take a bath?

Other children were afraid to get close to him. Once, an older boy pushed him. He fell and skinned both knees. The older boy yelled, "You're so dumb. You can't even talk!"

Children laughed, pointing at his tattered clothes and bare feet. "Beggar boy! Beggar boy! You're just a dirty beggar boy with rags for clothes."

The Stable Boy never fought back. He just looked at their clean clothes, fine sandals and washed faces. Then, he turned and walked away so they could not see his tears.

As darkness fell each night, wherever an empty stable could be found, the tired, dirty child would lay his head on the hay to cry himself to sleep and dream of his mama and the stories she had once told.

Now it came to pass in those days of King Herod that the Roman emperor, Caesar Augustus, ordered a census to be taken. Every person was to return to the home of his ancestors to be counted. People walked or rode donkeys to the little town of Bethlehem.

The Stable Boy saw new and different people. He wandered the streets. He listened to stories of faraway places. He heard news of kings and talk of the Messiah, who was said to be coming soon. *Could this be the Messiah my mama told me about? Won't matter to me if He does come. Nobody, 'specially a king, cares about somebody like me anyway.*

As the town became crowded, the boy began to feel afraid. Some strangers were rude. Some yelled at him to go away. He remembered an old innkeeper and his wife who had been kind to his mother. He felt he might be safe in their stable. Besides, his old friend Josephine lived there with lots of cats that would keep him warm on cold nights.

After dark, the boy wandered from street to alley and found the inn. Then he stood around the stable until he felt

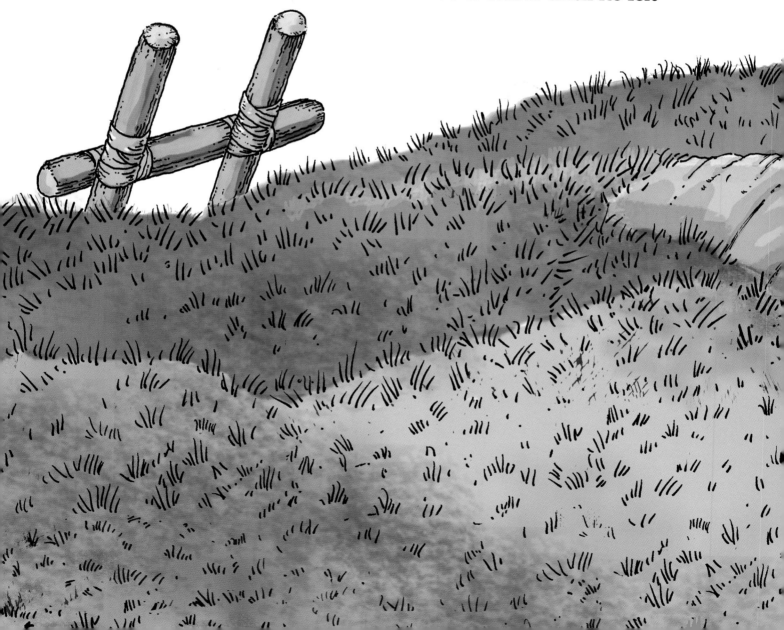

certain nobody was watching, opened the door and squeezed through, pulling it shut behind him. As he made his bed in the loft, he thought, *Now I won't have to be afraid. Nobody knows I am here, and if I hear somebody coming in, I'll just hide and be really quiet.*

The boy did not know that the innkeeper and his wife had watched from the back window of the inn as he entered their stable. Next morning, the innkeeper placed three empty water jugs just outside the stable door. Then he sat down on a wooden bench to rest. As he wiped the sweat from his face, he said, "If I had a son, I know he would help me with all these chores. But since God hasn't blessed me with a son, I guess I'll just come back later today and take these jugs to get water."

The old man got up and slowly walked back to the inn, wearing a sly smile. He knew all the while that the Stable Boy sat quiet as a mouse, listening to every word.

Poor man. He needs my help. I am strong, so I will surprise him, thought the Stable Boy. He scrambled down the ladder, watching for anyone who might discover his hiding place. One by one, he carried the jugs to the public well, filled them with water, and returned them to where the innkeeper had left them. By the time he finished, his little arms ached and his tummy growled with hunger. But his heart was filled with the warm contentment of helping another as he climbed back to the loft and slept soundly, snuggled in the hay with a purring cat.

Warm evening sunbeams woke the boy. He wondered how long he had been sleeping. After all, he usually slept at night. Suddenly he remembered why he had been so tired and rushed down the ladder to see if the water jugs were still there. To his great surprise, the water was gone and there, on the bench, was a neatly covered tray of food, complete with fresh milk. He gobbled up every single bite, sharing the milk with the kittens. He didn't see the innkeeper and his wife peeking out their back window, pleased to see a hungry boy eat so well.

For two weeks the innkeeper and his wife played a game of cat and mouse with the Stable Boy. Though they never saw each other face-to-face, the innkeeper sat on the bench every morning, placed a tray of food there, talked about the work he needed to do, and slowly walked back to the inn. The Stable Boy would then spend his day doing the best job a little boy could do to help his new friend. Every evening, he would find another good meal waiting on the bench.

One night, as the Stable Boy finished feeding the animals, he thought, *The nights are getting so cold. I hope all the kittens will sleep with me tonight and help me stay warm.*

To his surprise, his food was nice and warm, but that wasn't all. Laying next to his dinner was the most beautiful wool blanket his eyes had ever seen. He very carefully unfolded it, ran his fingers over the woven threads, and brushed its softness on his face.

As he turned to look toward the inn, his eyes met those of the innkeeper and his wife. For the first time since he became all alone in the world, he felt cared for. His dirty little face shone with tender gratitude that touched his new friends deeply, as a mysterious love and friendship had grown between the three people.

One night, just as the boy was almost asleep, he heard the stable door creak open. He listened as the innkeeper spoke. "With so many coming to count for the census, Bethlehem is overflowing with people looking for a place to stay. I am sorry that we have no room for you and your wife in the inn, but at least you can rest here. There is plenty of clean hay and water, and I will leave this candle to light the darkness for you. Oh yes," he added, "there is a small boy who lives here in the stable. He does not speak, but he is a very good boy, and he will not trouble you."

The husband thanked the inkeeper for his kindness and began to prepare a place for his wife to rest. He made her a bed of hay, covered it with a small blanket and helped her lie down.

"How are you doing?" he asked. "I know it's been a long journey, and you must be so very tired."

"Yes, my husband," she answered, "I am tired, but we have shelter here. We must rest and prepare for this child, as I feel the time for Him to arrive is very near."

As he poured water from the jar left by the innkeeper into a clay bowl, the man sat down on the hay by his wife and removed the sandals from her swollen feet. Washing her feet, he said, "Please, tell me again what the angel said to you. I love hearing his words."

She answered, "I understand. I, too, am overwhelmed by what I was told. The angel, Gabriel, called me 'favored one' and said the Lord is with me. I am not to be afraid, for I have found favor with God. I, a virgin, will bear a son and His name will be Jesus. The angel told me that Jesus will be great. The angel said Jesus will be called the Son of the most High. The Lord God will give to Him the throne of His ancestor David. He said the child will be holy and will be called Son of God … *the Son of God*, Joseph!"

"Yes," Joseph replied. "In my dreams, the angel of the Lord told me, just as you were told, to not be afraid to take you as my wife. The child, who will soon be born, is from the Holy Spirit. Like you, I was told to name Him Jesus, for He will save His people from their sins. All of this fulfills what has been spoken by the Lord through the prophets. We have nothing to fear for God is with us."

Mary became quiet for a few minutes then said, "I wonder how God will spread the good news of His Son throughout the world. Will He send His angels to every person?"

Joseph replied, "I don't know, but He will reveal the answer to us when the time is right. Of that, I am certain."

In the dark loft, the Stable Boy lay still as a rock. His heart was racing. He was excited at the secrets he heard. *They are talking about the Messiah—the Messiah my mama told me about? He is coming, just like she said. I must be dreaming.* The hour was late, and the tired, bewildered child closed his eyes and drifted off to sleep.

Long before the sun was up, a bright light, glowing like a thousand candles, woke the boy. The night was silent. A wondrous, holy presence filled the stable. Joseph and Mary felt it. The boy felt it. Even Josephine and the kittens opened their eyes and lifted their ears.

Something has happened, thought the boy as he slowly crept toward the ladder to peek below. His mouth dropped open in astonishment at what he saw. Lying in a manger, wrapped in swaddling clothes, was a beautiful newborn baby. Light from the child shone on Joseph and Mary as they silently adored Him. All the animals knelt in their places as they watched the baby.

The Stable Boy gasped for air, as the sight had taken his breath. *Oh! Oh, He has come. The Messiah King has come, and He did find me,* he thought.

As quietly as he could, he crept down the ladder. His bare feet hardly made a sound as he tipped toward the wooden feed bucket and spade hanging by the door. He eased the door open just enough to squeeze himself and the bucket through and made his way to a nearby hillside. Though it was still night, Bethlehem was alive with light from a bright and beautiful star that seemed to sit in the heavens, just above the stable.

Just as the sun peeked over the horizon, the boy returned to the stable, carrying the bucket, which held a small cedar tree. This time, the door creaked as he opened it wide. *Yes, He is still here. It wasn't a dream*, he thought. He slowly walked over and placed the bucket next to the manger that held the sleeping baby Jesus. He removed his precious blanket from his shoulders and spread it around the tree. There he knelt before the Christ child and bowed his little head. "Little boy, what have you brought to us?" asked Joseph.

Mary said, "The child does not speak. Remember what the innkeeper told us last night?"

The Stable Boy opened his dark eyes and looked into the eyes of Mary and Joseph, and finally at the sleeping baby. Then, for the first time in two years, he spoke. "This is the Messiah King. My mama told me He would come to save the world and He would bring hope and peace for all people, even for me. Mama said He would find me, and He did."

"Why did you bring Him this tree?" asked the man.

In a soft, low voice, the boy answered, "I heard that the cedar tree is the tree of royalty. This is my King, so I brought Him a royal tree and gave Him my blanket because I have nothing else to give."

Suddenly the innkeeper and his wife entered the stable.

He asked, "Who was it we heard speaking? Was it the boy?

Could it be?"

His wife asked, "Is this true? Did you speak, child?"

The boy did not know if this was good or bad as he replied,

"Yes, ma'am and I hope you won't be angry with me.

I gave baby Jesus my blanket. He is so special.

My blanket was all I had. Please forgive me."

"Oh, you precious boy," said the innkeeper's wife.

She hugged him until he could hardly breathe.

"Of course I forgive you. I will make you a new blanket,

one even better than before."

The innkeeper dropped to his knees, placed his hands on the boy's shoulders, and looked deeply into his beautiful, brown eyes. He said, "Son, you are so good and kind to others, just like your mama. She would be so proud of you. I am sorry you can no longer be with her, but you need a home and a family to care for you. And we need a son to fill our home with love and laughter. Will you help us make a new family, the three of us?"

The Stable Boy could say nothing. He just stood looking into the innkeeper's kind eyes in disbelief. Everyone waited for his answer.

Finally, the woman asked, "What is your name, child?"

When the boy did not answer, she said, "I am called Mary, and my husband is called Joseph. What name did your mama call you?"

He looked toward Mary and slowly answered, "Samuel. Samuel was the name Mama called me. But sometimes, when I was really good, she called me Sam. I loved when she called me Sam."

"Well, Samuel, come here," said Mary, reaching out to hold his small hand in her own. "Let me tell you some good news. All of us were created by our Father in heaven. That means you are already part of this man and woman's family.

"God has a plan for each of us, Samuel. Perhaps, He brought you to this place, so you can feel His love through these two kind people and you are supposed to be with them. What do you think?"

Samuel was so overwhelmed with joy and feelings of being loved and wanted that he simply could not speak. As tears streamed down his little brown cheeks, he ran to the innkeeper and wrapped his little arms around his neck. The man held him close as he wiped his own tears.

Samuel's new mother said, "Samuel, how about we go in and have a good breakfast and perhaps a nice warm bath and clean clothes? Then we'll come back here with food for our guests."

"Yes, Sam, let's go home," said the innkeeper.